This book belongs to

_____

The Surprising Knight

A Lesson in Loving Others

by Doug Peterson
Illustrated by Tod Carter and Joe Spadaford

SCHOLASTIC INC.
New York Toronto London Auckland Sydney
Mexico City New Delhi Hong Kong Buenos Aires

he castle buzzed with excitement and music. **"Ba-ba-ba! Bar-barian!"** sang a strolling pea with a mandolin. "You got me rocking and a rolling, baking and a cooking, Rhubarbarian!"

"I just love that serf music!" the Duke of Scone exclaimed.

"Me too," said Petunia, a Rhubarbarian princess.

Duke and Petunia had their eyes on the prize—and on the pies. They wanted to win the prize for the best pie in the kingdom. In fact, *everyone* wanted to win the Pie Prize, which was going to be given out at the Pie-Palooza Festival.

It was
the night before
the festival, and the castle
ovens were heating up. King Stanley
himself would be there the next day
to choose the Pie Prizewinner.
In the castle, the Hard Day's
Knight worked night and day on a
pecan pie. The Knight Owl stayed up
late working on his Black Forest pie.
And the Starry Knight created his
favorite—shepherd's pie.
As for Duke and Petunia . . .

8

BONK!

"Oops. My mistake," said Duke. He and Petunia had clunked heads while bending down to pick up their apple pie.

"No, my mistake. You first," Petunia said.

"No, you first," said Duke.

CLUNK!

They both went first and bonked heads for what had to be the fourteenth time that day.

BAM! BAM! BAM!

Very confused, Duke glanced at Petunia and asked, "Was that the sound of us clunking heads three more times?"

"No, I think it's the sound of someone knocking on the castle door," Petunia said, with a giggle.

Duke and Petunia looked down from the tower window. An old, old man banged on the door with his walking stick.

But none of the knights on the first floor would answer the door. They were too busy baking pies.

"Bah!" scoffed the Knight Watchman. "It's just an old man. I'm not letting *him* in."

BAM! BAM! BAM!

"How can they leave an old man out in the cold like that?" wondered Duke.

So Duke and Petunia scurried downstairs and pushed open the heavy wooden door.

12

BONK!

Duke and Petunia clunked heads bowing to the old man.

"Thank you, my children, for welcoming me,"
said the old man.

"Pull up ye olde recliner, while we get you some
milk," Duke said.

So the old man plopped in the chair, as Duke and
Petunia ran off to get him something to drink. The
old man watched the Wild Knight run around like a
crazy man and listened to the Knight at the Opera
sing while he baked.

Everyone was busy, but no one
was acting very nice.

"Out of my way!" shouted the
Hot Summer Knight.

"Work faster!" the Knight Before Last yelled at his assistant, Holly Berry.

Suddenly the Stormy Knight stormed into the dining room, throwing the door open without even looking. The door slammed into the Knight Watchman, knocking his pie right into his face.

SPLAT!

The Knight Watchman was furious! In fact, he was so
angry that he pushed over the huge table loaded with pies.
This made *everyone* angry! Furious, all of the knights
hurled pies at each other right and left.

SPLAT!

SPLAT!

SPLAT!

The Knight at the Opera tried to calm everyone with a little knight music. "I wish they all could be Rhubarbarian girls!" he sang. "Well, East Coast pies are—"

SPLAT!

(It's hard to sing with pie in your face.)

Pies were flying so wildly that one of them even smacked the old man square in the kisser.

SPLAT!

So Duke and Petunia
helped him upstairs
to safety.

19

CLUNK! Duke and Petunia bonked heads as
they both bent down to wipe pie from the old man's face.

"I can't believe they did this to you," said Petunia.
"How can we make it up to you?"

The old man eyed the apple pie that Duke and Petunia
had baked. "Well—I am a bit hungry," the old man said.

CLUNK!

Duke and Petunia looked at each other. They had spent all
day baking that pie for the contest! But they knew that God
would rather they feed a hungry man than win a silly prize.
"Dig in!" Duke shouted.

By morning, the entire castle

was a mess. It had been a frightful night of fighting.

Suddenly the Knight Watchman shouted, "The king is coming!"

Sure enough, a royal carriage was winding its way toward the castle.

The knights hurried to clean up the mess, but it was too little—too late.

All of the knights lined up in front of the
castle as king's carriage came to a stop. The
door swung open and out stepped . . .

. . . a pea?!?

"*Bonjour!*" shouted the king's helper, a pea named Jean-Claude.

"But where's King Stanley?" the Winter's Knight asked.

"Right behind you!" shouted a voice from the castle.

The knights spun around and nearly fainted. The old man, standing in the castle door, yanked off his hood. It was King Stanley!

"But . . . but . . ." The knights
did not know what to say.

"When you became knights, you promised to obey the most
important rule in our kingdom: to love God and love each other," King
Stanley said. "I wanted to find out if you really put your words into action."

To see if the knights would act lovingly, King Stanley had disguised himself
as an old man and arrived a night early. Unfortunately, the knights had not lived
up to their promise.

It was certainly a time for surprises. But the biggest surprise was what happened next.

King Stanley held up an empty pie pan for all to see. "**This** is the prizewinning pie!" King Stanley announced. "And the winners are Duke and Petunia!"

"But there's nothing in the pan," pointed out the Scary Knight.

"There's nothing in the pan because they shared this pie lovingly," said King Stanley. "That makes it the greatest pie of all!"

Now, Duke and Petunia did not win because their pie tasted the best or looked the best. They won because they showed their love for others. They won because they treated others like kings.

CLUNK!

So King Stanley handed Duke and Petunia the Pie Prize, and they bowed to the crowd. CLUNK!

It was one of those days.

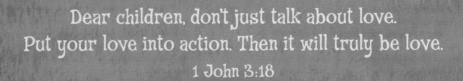

Dear children, don't just talk about love.
Put your love into action. Then it will truly be love.

1 John 3:18